6 25

**Safety Advice
for Kids**

stranger
danger

Safety Advice for Kids

stranger danger

Ellen Jackson

First Printing, September 1991

International Standard Book Number
0-88290-426-4

Horizon Publishers' Catalog and Order Number
1333

Printed and distributed
in the United States of America by

& Distributors, Incorporated
P.O. Box 490 Bountiful, Utah 84011-0490

Contents

1
No One Can Tell
Who Is a Dangerous Person

Strangers are all around. Most of them are nice. But
if you don't know someone, you should be careful.
Stephen, age 10

In today's society, many of the people you see every day are strangers. Usually these people ignore you and you ignore them. But once in awhile, someone you don't know may approach you in a friendly way. Unfortunately, some of these friendly people may not be what they seem.

Because "bad guys" are often shown on television as mean or poorly dressed or unfriendly, children and teenagers often think they can tell who is likely to be dangerous. But *no one* can tell who is a dangerous stranger, so it's a good idea to treat all strangers with caution.

Each year three out of every one hundred people in the United States are victims of a crime or an attempted crime. Most of these crimes are committed by a person who is a stranger to the victim. But crimes such as these *can* be prevented. This book will teach you ways to stay safe from strangers who may want to harm you.

You are not helpless. There are many ways to spot trouble before it happens. Do you know the difference between a stranger, an acquaintance, and a friend? Do you know how to protect yourself on the street and at home? Do you know what to do it you're approached by a stranger? In this book you will learn the answers to these and other questions you may have about stranger danger.

2
Who is a Stranger?

A stranger is someone you've never met. Someone
bad or someone good—you never know.
                              Ricardo, age 11

A *stranger* is *anyone* unfamiliar. It doesn't matter whether the person is big or little, young or old, male or female. It doesn't matter if the person is wearing a business suit or is dressed casually. A stranger is someone you haven't seen before or whose name you don't know.

Someone who means to harm you will try to win your trust. The following is a list of approaches strangers have used. A stranger might:

1. Say that your mother or father has been in an accident or is sick.

2. Ask personal questions to get information about you or your family.

3. Pretend to be a police officer or other figure of authority.

4. Pretend to need help of some kind. He or she may ask for directions or to use the phone.

5. Offer to show you something exciting or to give you a special treat.

6. Play a game such as basketball, baseball, or other sport with you and your friends.

Of course, not everyone who approaches you in one of these ways is a dangerous stranger, but you'll never know for certain. If a stranger tries to talk to you, the best thing to do is turn and walk away, hang up the phone, or tell a responsible adult. Never go with anyone, even someone who claims to be a police officer or claims to be someone sent by your parents, without telling a responsible adult first.

An *acquaintance* is someone you've seen before but still don't know much about. An acquaintance may be someone who lives in your neighborhood, a kid you know at school, a clerk who works in a store near your house, or anyone else you've seen around or talked to a few times.

In an emergency, you may need to ask an acquaintance for help. But don't mistake an acquaintance for a friend. Remember, you really don't know an acquaintance very well. If he or she does something that makes you feel uncomfortable or bad, get away and stay away. Then tell a responsible adult. You don't owe an acquaintance anything.

A *friend* is someone you know a great deal about. He or she is a person you or your parents have known for a long period of time—probably for at least a year. Usually you know your friend's family, and he or she knows your family. A friend doesn't do things that make you feel uncomfortable or bad. A friend is someone you can trust.

3
Be Aware

A man who had a burglar alarm company put leaflets on cars that read: "If you didn't see me put this on your windshield, I could just as easily have stolen your car." While he was doing this, someone stole his truck.

One out of four households was affected by crime in 1988. This does not mean that every neighborhood has a serious crime problem. Some neighborhoods have lots of crime while others have very little.

It's important to be realistically alert to stranger danger. Call your local library or police station to find out how bad crime is in your neighborhood. This information is often available to anyone who wants to ask for it. Then take *precautions* to prevent crime.

Be especially careful when you're in an *unfamiliar* part of town or out alone after dark. Studies done with criminals in prison show that these people choose their victims carefully. A criminal will stay away from someone who might put up a fight. A likely victim is someone who doesn't seem to be paying close attention to his or her surroundings, someone who is loaded down with packages, or someone who appears afraid or lacking in confidence.

You can use this information to protect yourself. When you walk down the street, are you aware of the people around you? If necessary, could you give a brief description of that stranger who passed you on your way to the store—or that stranger who sat behind you on the bus? Do you walk with an open, *confident* stride? The first thing you should do is practice walking in an alert manner. Look around from side to side, noticing everyone and everything.

When you return home, practice observing your house to see if everything seems normal. Would you notice if there were doors or windows standing open or if your belongings were scattered about? If such a thing should happen, you should go to a neighbor's house and call the police or your parents. You should never enter your house if you suspect an intruder might be inside.

Look at your home as a criminal would look at it. Are there *deadbolt locks* on all your outside doors? Do you keep all doors and windows locked? Do you have safety pins on the windows? Could any shrubs or trees around the house provide cover for someone trying to break in? Do you keep your garage locked? Are there outside lights near all doors? Can someone see into your house from the outside?

If you notice any problems, talk to your parents about making your house more *secure*. You can prevent a number of problems before they happen if you stay alert and aware.

4
On the Street

*Safety tip: when you're on a bus alone, always sit
as close as you can to the bus driver.*

When you are away from home, be especially cautious. Go places with friends whenever possible. Remember that a friend's friend may be only an acquaintance to you. If your best friend Steve wants you to ride home from school with his sister's boyfriend or his cousin's neighbor, say "no thanks." Don't accept rides from acquaintances.

When you are out on the street or walking to and from school, wear clothing that doesn't attract attention. Don't carry *personalized* belongings with your name and address on them. Don't wear expensive-looking clothes or flashy jewelry. Your shoes should allow you to run if you should need to do so, and your clothes should be loose enough to allow you to move freely. Don't load yourself down with unnecessary possessions.

Try not to carry large sums of money, but if for some reason you must do so, don't tell anyone how much you have. Carry emergency money with you, but put it in a special place—away from money you use for everyday purchases. Memorize two or three useful phone numbers, such as your parent's work phone or the number of a trusted neighbor, in case of emergency. Always carry your backpack or purse close to your body.

Don't talk to anyone who wants to start a conversation with you on the street. Keep walking and look away. If someone in a car asks for directions, stay far away and give quick directions or say that you don't know.

But what if someone needs help? Suppose a woman approaches you on the street and tells you that she has twisted her ankle and needs help getting home. In this case, you might offer to *send* help, to call a responsible adult, or to make an emergency phone call for her. But never put yourself in danger. Remember an adult should ask another *adult* for help whenever possible. It is not your responsibility to take care of a grownup.

If you think someone is following you, check first before you take action. Cross the street and walk back in the direction from which you came. If the person continues to follow you, walk as quickly as you can to a busy street or neighborhood and ask a store clerk for help. If you cannot get to a busy street, knock on the door of a nearby house and ask if someone will make a phone call for you. Do *not* go home. You don't want the person following you to know where you live.

If you walk along a certain route every day, try to spot *safety places* where you can go for help if necessary. These might include: a friend's house, a store where you know the clerk, a church, a playground where there is an after-school program, or a trusted neighbor's house.

Try to walk on well-traveled streets. Always take the safest route. Never take a shortcut if it goes through an alley, a field, a parking lot, or any other deserted place. Stay away from places where someone could be hiding—such as vacant buildings, areas with heavy shrubbery, or parking structures—especially if you are out after dark. *Vary* your routine so that no one who might want to harm you can predict where you will be at a certain time.

When someone hollers at you or insults you, pretend you don't hear and keep on walking. Head for a "safety place" if the problem continues. Walk facing traffic so no one can stop a car quickly and grab you from behind. In fact, it's a good idea to stay twenty or thirty feet away from any car with occupants.

Stay alert and you can often avoid trouble before it occurs. Maybe you're out walking one evening when you see a stranger coming toward you. There's no one else around, and you notice that the man is staring at you. Why take chances? A good *strategy* is to cross the street before you must pass him. Continue walking on the opposite side of the street until he is out of sight. Remember, avoid anyone who makes you feel uneasy.

If someone tries to attack you on the street, you must use your best judgment about what to do. If no weapon is involved and you are on a busy street, don't be afraid to attract attention. Yell and run away as fast as you can.

If a robber with a gun demands your money or jewelry, don't put up a fight. Cooperate and keep calm. Don't move suddenly. Announce what you are going to do before you do it. Say, "I'll give you my wallet. It's in my purse." Then reach for your wallet.

Play "what if" games when you are out alone. Ask yourself what you would do in different problem situations that might arise. The following are four "what if" situations for you to think about. There are no right answers, but some suggested solutions are listed at the end of this book.

What if?

1. You're on your way home from soccer practice, and you think someone is following you. You're walking down a busy street so you're safe for now, but your house is only five minutes away and you know that no one is home. What should you do?

2. You've been visiting a friend and now you're on the way home. You're walking down the street in an unfamiliar neighborhood when two older boys block your way. They won't let you pass and start calling you names. What should you do?

3. While you are in the park, an old woman stumbles and falls on the sidewalk in front of you. She seems to be unconscious. What should you do?

4. A man you've never seen lunges at you on the street. Another man chases him off, then offers to walk you home. What should you do?

5
Social Events

*Ancient superstition: to keep a stranger from harming
you, carry the right eye of a wolf in your right hand.*

It's sometimes hard to keep stranger danger in mind when you're going out to have a good time. But certain safety rules apply when you want to *socialize* with friends. Plan ahead, use good sense, and follow the who, what, and where rules listed below.

Who

It's a good idea to socialize mostly with friends. Don't accept dates or invitations from acquaintances unless you're going to be with a group of people.

Acquaintances can sometimes "feel" more familiar than they are. You may even refer to people you don't know well as "friends" if you've seen them around a number of times and if you go to the same school or belong to the same organizations.

Nevertheless, if you don't know someone well, make sure other people are around at all times. Or invite someone you would like to know better to your home when your family is there.

Don't let yourself be alone with an acquaintance. Unfortunately, "date rape" is a common occurrence these days. And rape can happen to boys as well as to girls. You don't want it to happen to you. The same thing is true about getting into a car with an acquaintance. Don't do it.

If you're out with someone who makes you feel uncomfortable, get away and call a friend or relative to come and get you. You don't need permission to use the telephone if you are frightened. Just pick it up and call.

Keep in mind that someone who likes you will never try to make you feel bad. If a person makes remarks about your appearance or touches you where you don't want to be touched, walk away quickly and stay away. Then tell an adult.

What

Don't go to a party if you don't know the people who are giving it. Try to find out ahead of time if you've been invited to a party involving tobacco, alcohol, or drugs. Don't go if the answer is "yes."

If, in spite of your best efforts, you are at a party where someone offers you alcohol or drugs, say "no thanks" and leave as quickly and quietly as possible. Don't let your date drive you home if he or she has been drinking or using drugs. Instead, call someone, or leave and take a bus or taxi home.

Always tell your parents exactly what time to expect you home. Make sure they have a phone number where you can be reached. Never bring large sums of cash to a social event, but don't forget your emergency money. Dress so that you don't stand out in the crowd.

Suppose you are at a school event or a rock concert and a woman you don't know approaches you. She says, "You don't know me, but I know your mother. Your father has been in an accident and your family is at the hospital. They asked me to come get you." What should you do?

Think before you act. Is there a friend who could drive you to the hospital? If you feel the woman is telling the truth, ask her where your father is and call the hospital to verify her story.

Suppose the woman says, "Your mother can't pick you up. She wants you to go to my house and she'll call you there." What should you do? You might call a trusted adult friend or relative and ask advice. You might ask the woman some questions to see if she really knows your mother, but be sure you ask *lots* of questions. Remember, it is fairly easy for someone to get personal information about you and your family. Even so, don't go with her without checking with a responsible adult first.

The best way to handle a situation like this, however, is with a *code word*. You and your parents should pick a word that is only known to members of the family. The word should be unusual enough that no one is likely to guess it, but a word that you can remember. That way, if your parents need to send someone to come and get you, they can tell the person the code word. Never tell your code word to *anyone*.

What if a policeman approaches you and asks you to go with him because someone in your family has been hurt? Ask him to show you some *identification*. Then ask him to show the identification to a supervising adult. If there is no one who can help, ask him to call another officer to come and verify his identification. Criminals have been known to pose as law enforcement officers, so don't assume that someone in a uniform is a person you can trust. A real police officer won't mind if you check his or her *credentials*. Try to get a good look at any stranger who tries to take advantage of you in any way. And don't forget to get a license number if you can.

Where

When you go out with friends, be sure you know ahead of time where you will be and how you will get there. Who will be driving? Is it someone you can trust? How will you be getting home? Make sure you have a *second* way of getting home in case of emergency. This is especially important if you will be in an unfamiliar or high-crime neighborhood. Never hitchhike, either alone or with a friend.

If you will be going by car, make sure the doors are locked and windows are rolled up before you start. On your way home, look inside before you get into the empty car. Look, especially, into the backseat area. Don't leave your purse, wallet, or anything valuable in plain view. If you think someone is following you and your friends, drive to a busy area or to the local police station.

Don't go home! Always be sure you lock the doors and roll up the windows when you leave the car—even for a few minutes.

If your car should break down, don't leave it to try and get help. Stay with the car, put the hood up, and lock the doors. Try to attract the attention of a passing motorist and ask him or her to call your parents or a taxi.

Going door-to-door to collect money or sell items for an organization presents special problems. Try to stay in your own neighborhood where you know some of the people. It's a good idea to go with a friend, and never, never go inside a stranger's house.

What if?

5. You have just started going to Midbury Middle School. You've finally been invited to a party, and at the party you notice that everyone is drinking beer. "Have some beer," says your new friend Dave. "My brother bought us a six pack and some pizza." What should you do?

6. Your friend Lisa offers to give you a ride home from school. When you meet her after school, she says, "My Aunt Regina's stepson is going to drive us home." What should you do?

7. You're at a school basketball game and a man comes up to you and says, "You don't know me but I work with your father. He's had a heart attack, and they've just taken him to the emergency room. Your mother will call us at my house. Come with me." What should you do?

8. You've just been shopping with your older sister. It's after dark and your sister has parked the car on the fifth level of a tall parking structure. You notice that a woman seems to be following the two of you as you walk toward your car. What should you do?

9. You're riding down in an elevator with a group of strangers. One by one everyone gets off until at the fourth floor you are left alone with a man who makes you feel uneasy. You still need to ride down to the first floor. What should you do?

6
Home Alone

Fascinating fact: about two million children are left alone in the house for part of each day in the United States.

When you're home alone, *never* let any stranger inside. If someone comes to the door, speak to the person through the door itself. A door chain will not prevent a determined criminal from forcing entrance to your house, so don't chain the door and then open it just a little.

If a stranger wants to speak to your parents, say, "My dad's asleep. If you leave your name and phone number, I'll have him call you when he wakes up." Say this even if you live alone with your mother. Never admit you're alone without an adult.

Even if someone says he or she has been sent to make repairs or deliver furniture or equipment, check with a parent before you let the person come in. You may need to phone your mother or dad at work. If you can't reach a parent, ask for the name of the agency, shop, or store that sent the person. Ask that he or she slip identification under the door. Then call and check to see if a delivery or repair person was supposed to come to your house.

If all this sounds like a lot of trouble, remember that criminals often use this method to gain entrance to a house or apartment. Don't take your safety and the safety of your family for granted.

If a stranger says he or she needs to deliver a package and you must sign for it, ask that the papers be slipped under the door. Then ask the person to set the package down and leave. Wait until you are alone before opening the door. Call the police if someone won't leave after being asked to do so.

Sometimes an adult may come to the door who seems to know your parents. The rules are the same. Don't let the person in. Don't let him or her know that your parents aren't home. Call your parents, if possible, and let your mother or father handle the situation.

7
Telephone Smarts

Fascinating fact: a house in Texas was stolen right off its foundation in 1980.

When you're home alone and the telephone rings, you still need to keep stranger danger in mind. If someone asks to speak to one of your parents, don't say that your mother and father aren't home. Say that your parents are busy, asleep, or in the shower. Never give personal information about your family to anyone. Sometimes burglars use this method to check out which homes to burglarize.

If someone calls and tells you he or she is taking a survey or that you or your family have won a prize, don't be fooled into giving out personal information. Ask the person to call back later when your parents can come to the phone.

Hang up on obscene phone calls or other telephone calls from strangers that disturb you in any way. If the person continues to harass you, call the police.

What if?

10. A woman comes to your door when you're home alone. She says she is your neighbor—the one who's just moved in across the street. She says the mail carrier accidentally left some of your family's mail in her mailbox and she wants to give it to you. You haven't met the new neighbor, but the woman does seem to know your mom's and dad's names. What should you do?

11. A little boy knocks on your door when you're home alone. He's crying and says that he's lost. What should you do?

12. The phone rings when you're home alone. When you pick it up, there's no one on the line. You hang up, but the same person calls back. You say "hello," but no one answers. This happens several times. What should you do?

8
Sexual Abuse

Fascinating fact: men are victimized by strangers three times more often than women.

It is estimated that at least one in four girls and one in ten boys will be sexually abused before the age of eighteen. An abuser can be a stranger or an acquaintance—even, sometimes, a person you think of as a friend.

Some children and young people think that adults should always be obeyed. This isn't true. You should feel free to say "no" to any adult who is touching you in an uncomfortable or confusing way. Remember, your body belongs to *you*. You have the right to refuse to touch or be touched. You shouldn't be embarrassed by this. It's quite possible to like a person but not want to be touched by him or her.

Sexual abuse can happen in many ways. People who abuse children have serious problems and need professional help. If you are a victim of abuse or attempted abuse, you should never feel bad or guilty about what has happened.

Remember that it is against the law for anyone to ask you to touch his or her private parts or for someone to try to touch yours. If this should happen to you:

1. Say "no" and push the person's hands away.

2. Leave immediately.

3. Tell a responsible adult.

4. Sometimes an adult will not believe you when you try to report abuse. If this should happen, find another adult to tell. Keep reporting until you find an adult who will believe you.

Report any adult who asks you to keep a "secret" about which you feel uncomfortable. If someone you don't know tries to give you gifts or money, or threatens your family, always report it. If a stranger tries to take your picture, tell your parents or a teacher. And don't forget that you always have the right to use the telephone to call for help if you're away from home and feeling uncomfortable.

What if?

13. You and your family are visiting your parent's friends, Mary and Bill. You haven't seen them in a long time. Bill says, "Come here, Karen. Give me a hug." You like Bill, but you don't want to hug him. For one thing, he has a scratchy beard. What should you do?

14. Your next-door neighbor tries to put his hands on your private parts. You push him away, but then he says, "If you tell your parents, I'll hurt your dog." What should you do?

15. During school your music teacher exposes himself and asks you to touch his private parts. You leave and tell your teacher, but she just says, "What? I don't believe you. Poor Mr. Richardson wouldn't do something like that."

Be Aware

Answer the following questions to see how aware of your surroundings you are.

1. You've seen pennies, nickels, dimes, and quarters many times. Each of these coins has a picture of someone on it. But on only one of these coins is the person facing *right*. Which coin has someone facing right? Who is it?

_____

_____

2. Every traffic signal has three lights—yellow, red, and green. Which one is on top?

_____

_____

3. What did you have for lunch yesterday?

_____

_____

4. What is the lowest number on your oven dial?

_____

_____

5. What number on your telephone has no letters that go with it?

_____

_____

6. How many electric outlets are in your bathroom?

_____

_____

9
What If (Answers)

1. First, be sure the person is *really* following you. Walk around the block, or suddenly turn and go back the way you came. If the person is still behind you, walk into a store and ask the store clerk if you can use the phone to call your parents or the police. Don't go home!

2. Try to ignore them. Don't get into an argument. Walk calmly back in the direction of your friend's house. Or if you feel you're in danger, you might try pretending that you live in a nearby house. Go to the door of the house, knock, and ask the person living there to call for help. While it usually isn't a good idea to talk to any stranger, sometimes you do need to ask someone you don't know for help if you're in a dangerous situation.

3. Ask someone to stay with the old woman and go for help. You shouldn't try to move her. Find a store clerk or park maintenance worker and ask him or her to call 911. Although you need to watch out for strangers, it is also important to help someone in need if you can do it safely.

4. This is an trick often used by criminals to gain the trust of an unsuspecting victim. *Don't* allow the second man to walk you home. Thank him, and then walk off by yourself.

5. This is a difficult situation. Everyone wants to have friends, and it's often hard to stand up to peer pressure. The best thing to do is to get away as quickly and as quietly as possible. You might call someone to come get you. Or if that's not possible, just say "no thanks" to the beer. Above all, don't drive with anyone who's been drinking.

6. Aunt Regina's stepson is a stranger to you so say "no thanks." Even if you know Aunt Regina and she's someone you trust, that doesn't mean her stepson is trustworthy too.

7. If you and your family have a code word, now is the time to use it. If your family doesn't have a code word, ask the man where your father is. Call the hospital and verify the man's story. Tell the man you need to talk with a family friend first. Call someone who knows your family well and ask him if he knows who the man is and if you should go with the man. Don't make the mistake of being so concerned about your dad that you forget stranger danger.

8. Don't go to the car. Leave the parking structure and find a store or public phone booth in a busy, well-lighted place. Call someone to come get you.

9. Trust your feelings. Get off at the fourth floor and wait for the man to leave. Or take the stairs down to the first floor. Don't be trapped alone with someone you don't trust in an elevator, public rest room, or any other place.

10. Don't let the woman inside your home just because she knows your parents' names. Ask her to put the mail in the mailbox, or have her leave it under the doormat. When she's gone, you can retrieve it.

11. Criminals sometimes use children to help them gain a victim's trust. Don't be fooled. At the same time, it *is* important to help other people whenever possible. You might call a neighbor or the police. You could also ask the boy (through the closed door) for his telephone number and call his parents from your phone.

12. Keep hanging up. The other person on the line will probably get bored and stop calling. If the calls continue, call the police.

13. You should try to handle the situation without hurting Bill's feelings, if possible, but the most important thing to remember is that *you* have the right to choose whether to touch or not to touch. This is true for all kinds of touches. You might offer to shake hands with Bill and let him know you're glad to see him, but insist on your rights.

14. Say "No!" Leave his house immediately, tell your parents, and call the police. The best way to protect yourself from any threat is to tell the authorities about it.

15. Tell another teacher or even the principal. Keep telling people until you're believed.

Glossary

ACQUAINTANCE: Someone you've seen before or talked to but still don't know well.

CAUTION: The act of being careful and avoiding danger.

CODE WORD: A secret word that a family uses to identify someone who's been sent to help in an emergency.

CONFIDENT: Sure of oneself; alert and at ease.

CREDENTIALS: Certificate or identification that says a person has certain authority.

DEADBOLT LOCK: A bolt that is moved into place by the turning of a knob or key.

FRIEND: Someone you or your family has known for a long time and can trust.

IDENTIFICATION: Something such as a badge or a card by which a person's authority can be established.

PERSONALIZED: To have had something marked with someone's name or initials.

PRECAUTIONS: Measures taken beforehand against possible danger.

SAFETY PLACES: Places picked out along a route where a person can find help in case of danger.

SECURE: Free from danger.

SOCIALIZE: To take part in a party, gathering of friends, or other entertainment involving people.

STRANGER: Someone you haven't seen before or someone whose name you don't know.

STRATEGY: A plan or method to reach a goal.

UNFAMILIAR: Not well-known; strange.

VARY: To do something in a different way; to change.

VICTIMS: People who are harmed or suffer some loss.

Bibliography

Anderson, Deborah and Martha Finne, *Michael's Story*, Dillion Press, Inc. 1986.

Anderson, Deborah and Martha Finne, *Liza's Story*, Dillion Press, Inc. 1986.

Brown, Gene, *Keeping Your Kids Safe: A Handbook for Caring Parents*, Cloverdale Press, Inc. 1985.

Ebert, Jeanne, *What Would You Do If. . . .; A Safety Game for You and Your Child*, Houghton Mifflin Co., 1985.

Ellwood, Ann and Carol Orsag Madigan, *The Macmillan Book of Fascinating Facts*, Macmillan Publishing Co., 1989.

Jackson, Ellen and Ann Panizzon, *Stay on the Safe Side*, Governor's Youth Crime Prevention Program (California), 1987.

Kraizer, Sherryll Kerns, *The Safe Child Book*, Dell Publishing Co., Inc., 1985.

Kyte, Kathy S., *Play It S.A.F.E.: The Kids' Guide to Personal Safety and Crime Prevention*, Alfred A. Knopf, 1983.

Leiner, Katherine, *Both My Parents Work*, Franklin Watts, 1986.

Long, Lynette and Thomas, *The Handbook for Latchkey Children and Their Parents*, Arbor House, 1983.

Quiri, Patricia Ryon and Suzanne I. Powell, *Stranger Danger*, Julian Messner, 1985.

Schwartz, Alvin, *Cross Your Fingers, Spit In Your Hat*, J.B. Lippincott Co., 1974.

Sobol, Donald J., *Encyclopedia Brown's Third Record Book of Weird and Wonderful Facts*, William Morror and Co., 1985.

Terkel, Susan N. and Janice E. Rench, *Feeling Safe and Strong: How to Avoid Sexual Abuse and What to Do If It Happens to You*, Lerner Publications Co., 1984.

Vogel, Carole G. and Kathryn A. Goldner, *The Dangers of Strangers*, Dillion Press, Inc., 1983.